AUTHOR'S FOREWORD

The first time I saw Nikolai in the crowded school yard I was drawn to him. He seemed in a world of his own. He saw me, then quickly turned away. That did it. I had to find out more about him. It was hard going. Ever so slowly, I discovered a little boy with a world of big dreams. The same could also be said about Denmark, a little country which has grown up with big dreams. But that is the story of Nikolai which you will discover for yourself.

You will find in the story some Danish words with vowels unknown in English. They are the three vowels æ, ø, and å.

æ sounds like the vowels in "egg" and "air."
ø is similar to the vowel in "hurt" and "blur."
å is a deep "a", somewhat like the "a" in "all" and "awe."

NIKOLAI
THE BOY WHO RAN AWAY
Photos by Douglas Blackwood
© Copyright 1987 by Scandinavia
Publishing House, Nørregade 32,
DK-1165 Copenhagen K.
English-language edition first published 1988
through special arrangement with Scandinavia
jointly by Wm.B. Eerdmans Publishing Co.,
255 Jefferson Ave. S.E. Grand Rapids, Michigan 49503

Printed in Hong Kong

ISBN 0-8028-5025-1

NIKOLAI
The Boy Who Ran Away

Douglas Blackwood

Photos by Douglas Blackwood

William B. Eerdmans Publishing Company

Grand Rapids, Michigan

"I don't want to go to school!" Nikolai shouted so loudly everyone in the flat could hear him.

"Will you stop shouting!" his mother said, taking a firm hold of his arm. "I know how you feel. But shouting won't help you."

"But **Mor**, Lars is always picking on me. He's a real bully!"

"Try to be friends with Lars instead of always fighting."

"He's the one who starts it! I don't do anything and...."

"Yes, I know. Come on now, Nikolai. We'll talk about it later when **Far** gets home."

"No, don't do that. Please don't tell **Far**." Nikolai's father, a ship's captain, was very strict. Sometimes Nikolai did not see him for days when he was away at sea.

"All right then," **Mor** agreed. "Now hurry up or you'll miss the school bus. Have you got something for the school's 'give-away'?"

"What give-away?" Nikolai had been so upset about Lars that he had forgotten.

"Really Nikolai!" His mother frowned. "The give-away for the refugee children." Nikolai remembered then that his school was collecting clothes and toys. The refugees, Nikolai had learned, had escaped from their own country because of war. Many had come to Denmark hoping to start a new life. "Why not give away some of your toys. You have so many you don't use anymore. Now get off to school, quickly!" **Mor** had to feed Nikolai's baby sister, Mette.

Nikolai opened a large box filled with toys. Inside was a train set, hundreds of Lego pieces, cars, games, and puzzles. Nikolai found nothing he wanted to give away. "There must be some old socks in the drawer," he thought. He stuffed several pairs in his bag and headed down the stairs.

Outside, the frosty morning air stung Nikolai's face. The snow had melted away as it did in Denmark during the spring. Nikolai lived in an old part of Copenhagen, the capital city. The street, except for a few people on bicycles, was quiet. In Copenhagen just about everyone had a bicycle. The city was very flat.

Nikolai followed the street alongside a canal lined with old boats and barges. On one boat which was painted red and had not been used for years, Nikolai had built a little hiding place. He often played there alone. His little corner was hidden away below the deck so no one else could find it.

"Oh no!" whispered Nikolai as he suddenly caught sight of Lars and three other bullies at the bus stop. He hurried and hid himself below a bridge. His heart was pounding. The boys stood directly over him. He could hear every word they said. Lars was bragging about himself again.

The more Nikolai listened to the boys, the more he realized Lars was planning something.

"We won't get caught if we do it after school," Lars said.

"But aren't the things locked away?" another boy asked nervously.

"I know a window that doesn't lock properly. There are boxes full of good things. No one would know if some were missing," Lars said as the school bus pulled up. The boys got on. Nikolai waited until the bus had gone before climbing out. He thought about what Lars had said, but did not know enough to figure out the plan.

Since he had missed the school bus, Nikolai decided to go back home. When he reached the red boat, he stopped. His secret corner was inside a hatch. He climbed down a ladder below the deck. Some light came inside through a small skylight. Inside, Nikolai had built a table and bench out of planks. There was a porthole, and the water lapped softly outside. All the while, the more Nikolai thought about Lars the unhappier he became. He wished someone understood him. "**Far** never talks to me," he sulked. "**Mor** cares about Mette more than me." He felt cold and alone. The rocking of the boat made him sleepy. He curled up on the bench and drifted to sleep.

Sometime later, the boat jolted. Nikolai woke up. He did not know how long he had been asleep. He remembered a dream about a Viking ship. In his dream, Nikolai had worn a helmet with horns and had a long sword. He had sailed to Fyn or one of the hundreds of islands in Denmark. A thousand years ago the Viking oakwood fighting ships had travelled as far away as Iceland, Greenland, and America. Nikolai loved all the stories he had heard about the Vikings. There were so many heroes like Thor, the god of thunder and lightning, and monsters like the giant sea serpent Midgard. Nikolai wished he had lived in the time of the Vikings. Then he had the idea of running away. He had once read an exciting story about a boy who hid on a ship and travelled to many lands. But that was just a story. He wondered how he could do it himself. "If only this boat could sail," Nikolai muttered. But it needed too much repair work. "There's got to be another boat somewhere. But where?" He reached for his bag and climbed on deck.

The sun was high up. Nikolai's eyes were half closed with sleep. After a few minutes he started off in the direction of the city.

He hurried past many grand buildings and monuments. There was the beautiful Christiansborg Castle where the Danish government, called the **Folketing**, met. Nikolai did not stop to look. He was thinking too much about finding a boat. By now he had forgotten all about school.

The narrow streets of Copenhagen were crowded with shoppers. They did not notice Nikolai walking alone. At a fountain there was a noisy group of teenagers drinking beer. The shoppers kept well away from them.

"Come here, kid!" one of them shouted to Nikolai. He tried to sneak away. "Didn't you hear me? Come here!" A curly-haired youth shouted again and walked over to Nikolai.

He grabbed Nikolai by the collar, but another young man shouted, "Leave him alone! Can't you see he's scared?"

The first man let go of him and Nikolai was about to run off when the other came to him and asked, "Why aren't you at school?"

"I don't feel like it," Nikolai mumbled. "I can go where I want, can't I?" He tried to look big but the young man just shook his head.

"I ran off, too. But that doesn't make things easier. You just get more problems and meet up with a lot of weird people."

Then he left Nikolai and walked away slowly. Nikolai ran until he was out of breath. When he stopped he thought he heard the sound of drums beating.

The noise grew louder. Coming around the corner was a regiment of the Queen's Bodyguard. They were marching, as they did every day, to Amalienborg Palace, where Denmark's Queen, Dronning Margrethe II, lived. Denmark's line of kings and queens was the oldest in Europe. Nikolai admired the guards' tall bearskin hats and uniforms. His father had once been a Queen's Bodyguard, too, before Nikolai was born. For a moment he thought of returning home, but fear of his father's anger made him change his mind. Nikolai thought running away would make him braver. When the guards had marched past he crossed the street and kept going.

Beside a newspaper stand Nikolai saw a sign: 'Ship for the homeless in Copenhagen.'

"Where's that ship?" he asked the man at the stand.

"Down by the **havn**. It's full of refugees. From all over the world. There's no room for them anywhere else."

Nikolai remembered again about how his school was collecting things for refugees in Denmark. That they were living on a ship made him all the more curious. Nikolai knew his way around the **havn**, or harbor. He had watched the big car ferries come and go between Copenhagen and nearby Sweden.

At the dock Nikolai saw the ship. Several dark-skinned people who did not look Danish were walking onboard. Nikolai followed them up the gangplank.

"Hello. What do you want?" asked one girl. "Are you a refugee, too?" Her Danish was not very good.

"I...I've run away from home," Nikolai said, blushing.

The girl giggled. "Then you're a kind of refugee. My name is Mina."

13

'**Mina.**' The name had a nice sound. Her dark eyes looked mysterious. "Why did you come to Denmark?" Nikolai asked.

"Because my mother and I are Christians. My uncle was tortured and killed because he believed in Jesus. That's why my father helped us to escape, but he had to stay behind himself."

"Tortured and killed! Just for believing in Jesus!" Nikolai exclaimed. "Do you mean the Jesus that **jul** is about?" **Jul**, or Christmas, to Nikolai was the best time of the year with **brune kager**, gingerbread, and **julegrød**, rice porridge.

"Yes. Christmas is not allowed in my country. In Denmark you are free to believe and say what you want. Isn't that right?"

"Err... I've never thought about that," Nikolai replied.

"And Denmark is also one of the richest countries in the world," Mina said. "So why are you running away?"

"Oh... it's nothing compared to your reason." He told Mina about Lars the bully and about his father, who was always so busy.

"But at least you've got him at home with you. I haven't heard from my father in months. We had to leave everything behind to escape here."

"It must be hard being a refugee," Nikolai said.

"My school is holding a collection for refugees. Danish kids have so many toys. At school we've got boxes full of toys to give away...." Nikolai gasped. "Oh no! Lars is going to steal the give-away toys!" All of a sudden he had worked out Lars' plan, which he had overheard that morning.

"Steal what?" Mina asked, puzzled by Nikolai's worried look.

"I can't explain now. I've got to tell **Mor**. Can you call me soon?" He scribbled down his name and phone number on a piece of paper, then ran down the gangplank.

Mina looked at the note and waved. "I'll call," she shouted after Nikolai.

Nikolai ran almost all the way home. He had to stop Lars. He saw his mother standing by the red boat. "Nikolai!" she called out. "Where have you been? The school rang. I thought you must have been hiding on the red boat. Are you all right?"

"**Mor**!" Nikolai panted. Then he saw his father waving a long stick.

"I'll make sure you don't miss school again!" His face was red with anger.

"Lars made me miss the bus!" Nikolai gasped. Quickly, between deep breaths, he told them about Lars' plan to steal some of the give-away toys.

"We'll have to tell the school!" his mother said when he had finished.

"But don't tell them I told you," Nikolai pleaded.

"Lars will hurt me."

"You can't let Lars make you so scared all the time," his father said. "You will have to tell the teacher yourself."

The whole way while his mother drove him to school, Nikolai worried. He was sure Lars would find out who had told on him. When they arrived his mother had to drag him from the car. Nikolai refused to speak to the teacher. Finally, it was **Mor** who had to tell Nikolai's teacher about Lars' plan. Lars watched them from across the class. Nikolai was so afraid that he hid behind the door. The teacher thanked Nikolai, but he only wanted to go home.

All that night, Nikolai could not sleep. He tossed and turned — he was so nervous.

"**You** look like you need some fresh air, Nikolai!" his mother said, late the following morning. "Why don't you help Niels and me shop at the **torv**." Niels was Nikolai's older brother.

It was Saturday. "No school today," Nikolai thought, cheering up. He was tired from lack of sleep and very hungry. He made himself some **smørrebrød**, an open-faced rye bread sandwich. On one slice he laid ham topped with Danish Havarti cheese. He covered the other with cod's roe and remoulade sauce. He ate both in less than a minute.

"That's better!" he said, rubbing his tummy. The others were already waiting at the door.

The **torv**, or marketplace, was packed. "**Fem æbler for ti kroner**," called out a man selling apples. **Mor** bought ten. She handed over a twenty-kroner note. Nikolai still felt hungry. He bought a **ristet pølse**, a grilled Danish hot dog. The strong mustard, **sennep**, shot up the back of his nose. He sneezed and coughed, which made Niels laugh.

The two boys stopped at a bookstall. Nikolai found a comic book about Woden, a Viking god. The day of the week called Wednesday was named after him. Niels flipped through a story by Hans Christian Andersen, Denmark's most famous storyteller.

Nikolai looked up from his comic book. Suddenly his face fell. Lars was there, pushing his way through the crowd. "I don't want Lars to see me!" Nikolai squealed. He hid behind his brother, then ran and grabbed **Mor** around the waist. "I want to go, Lars is here," he said, pulling her by the coat.

"What am I going to do with you?" she sighed. Nikolai knew what he wanted to do. That was to leave quickly, very quickly.

"I hate Lars," Nikolai shouted, over the roar of the traffic. "I wish a car would run over him."

"Nikolai, the more you hate Lars, the more afraid of him you'll be," **Mor** said. "Hating never helps. You have to try to forgive him."

"How can I forgive him? He's terrible. He's the most awful person in the world."

"To forgive someone who badly hurts you is never easy. Lars may hurt you again. But hatred harms you more than him."

Nikolai pictured the curly-haired man who had grabbed him by the fountain. He remembered the angry look in the man's eyes.

"I don't want to hate," Nikolai said. "It hurts inside my tummy when I hate. But Lars won't stop."

A loud bus roared past them. "It's very noisy here," **Mor** said. "We'll go somewhere quiet to talk." So they continued down the road to a little park with a church.

"Let's go inside," she said.

The heavy church doors creaked open. When they shut behind them, the traffic noise was locked outside. No one was there. It was still. Nikolai and Niels felt they should whisper. Although Denmark had many big churches, Nikolai did not go to church, though Mother sometimes did.

The family all sat down together. **Mor** put her arm around Nikolai. "If you can't find peace in your heart to forgive Lars, then you have to ask God to give you peace."

"How does God give peace?" Nikolai asked.

"Ask Him to clean out the bad feeling, the angry voices inside you. Then ask Him to fill you up with peace."

Below the statue of an angel, Nikolai prayed, "I'm sorry for hating Lars. I can't help myself. Please, God, give me peace...."

The family sat quietly in the church for some time. The busy, noisy street outside seemed far away. Nikolai felt a quietness filter through his body to his hands and feet. Already he felt better inside.

Mor broke the silence by suggesting something which made both boys quite excited. "Above the church is a bell tower which looks over the whole city. Shall we go up?"

They went through a door and climbed a steep, narrow, wooden staircase. It rose up between several enormous bells. Finally it came outside and kept spiraling around the tower, high above Copenhagen. At the top, they were all puffing heavily.

"I can see Mina's ship down there!" Nikolai said, peering between the railings. The white ship was in the distance.

"Whose ship?" Niels asked.

Nikolai realized he had not told anyone about Mina.

"Mina's ship," he said. "She's a refugee who ran away with her mother." And he told them about how he had met her. His mother and brother peered down at the ship, wondering if they should believe Nikolai.

While Nikolai was telling his story, his brother kept interrupting, repeating words like 'Tortured!' 'No **jul**!' 'Escaped!'

"Mina seems to be quite a girl," **Mor** said when Nikolai had finished. "I would like to meet her."

"Her family has had a hard life," Nikolai said. "Mina helped me know how lucky I am."

"I don't think you would have said that an hour ago," Mother said.

"I know. I wish I was better."

"Nikolai," **Mor** said, smiling; "I couldn't be happier with you than I am just now."

Nikolai knew he felt different. He had changed on the inside, which was something only God could have done for him.

Several days later, Nikolai got a phone call from Mina.

"I received news about my father today," she said. "Can I come and see you?"

"Sure. Is he coming to Denmark?" Nikolai asked.

"No. He can't." Mina began to cry. "He's dead."

Nikolai's face turned white. "He was killed for helping me to escape." Nikolai heard her sobbing. Then the phone clicked and cut off.

Nikolai's heart sank right down into his stomach. He had never felt so sad before. He cried when he told **Mor**.

About an hour later, a taxi pulled up outside and out stepped Mina and her mother. Nikolai saw Mina's eyes were red and puffy. She wore a brave smile, though. Nikolai and Mina went for a walk in the sun while their mothers went inside. They wandered down to the canal. Nikolai showed Mina the red boat which he loved so much. They went onboard and sat with their legs dangling over the side. They watched a white duck swim past.

"I miss my **Far** so much," Mina said softly. "I don't know what I will do."

"God is like a **Far**," Nikolai said. "I asked Him to clean out all the anger and fear inside me."

Mina looked at Nikolai. Together they watched the sun sparkle on the water for a while without talking until it was time for them to go.

On their way home the children followed the canal past a clock tower to where it flowed under a bridge. A boy was throwing stones from the bridge into the water. Nikolai saw it was Lars. "That's the bully," he whispered to Mina.

 "Let's go the other way."

 Lars looked around and saw Nikolai and Mina. Nikolai clenched his fists expecting Lars to start a fight. But Lars only turned away. He lamely dropped his last stone into the water.

 "He's been crying," Mina said. Nikolai, too, had seen the sad look on Lars' face. They walked closer.

 "I could punch you for what you did to me at school," Lars said. "Aren't you scared?"

 Nikolai felt brave enough to tell him the truth.

 "I was afraid." Lars smiled a little. "Does fighting make you feel better?" Nikolai asked. Lars did not answer. "I'm not much better than you, though, Lars," Nikolai said. "You wanted to steal, but I kept all my things just for myself."

 "You've got it easy!" Lars said angrily. "My mother's drunk all the time. I can't go home without her screaming at me." Nikolai saw Lars was trying very hard not to cry. For the first time Nikolai thought he and Lars might actually become friends.

 Nikolai picked up two stones and walked up to Lars. "Take one," he said.

 Lars said nothing, but took the stone. The two boys threw the stones as far as they could. They splashed almost together. The boys chuckled. Mina saw a twinkle in Nikolai's eye which made her smile.

 Just then a loud dong echoed through the street. The children looked up at the clock tower. And from the distance, across the city famous for its many towers, came the sound of more bells.

 "Come on Lars and Mina," Nikolai said. "I want to show you my secret corner." Together the three walked to the old, red boat.

A week passed. Nikolai's father was away at sea. Lars met Nikolai at the bus stop every day and together they travelled to school. After school Lars helped Nikolai rebuild his corner on the boat.

Mina and her mother moved from the ship into an apartment of their own. Lars and Nikolai brought them a box of clothes and toys from Nikolai's school.

One night Nikolai came home and saw his father's jacket hanging up. Sure enough, **Far** was there, reading a newspaper. Nikolai tiptoed past him.

"I hear you and Lars are now friends," **Far** said. Nikolai nodded.

"Good! By the way, I've got something you might like to see. I've kept it stored away since I left the Queen's Bodyguard. Would you like to see my sword?" Nikolai jumped with excitement. He had not forgotten the time he saw the Queen's Bodyguard march past. **Far** opened a drawer and unwrapped the sword.

It was long and curved and glistened. Niels ran into the room to look, too. "A bodyguard's duty is to guard the palace," **Far** said. "I remember standing for hours even in the snow. I felt proud of Denmark. We are a small country, yet many other countries look to Denmark as an example of freedom. Never misuse your freedom, boys. Use it to help others." Nikolai held the sword carefully. It was very sharp. "Tomorrow," **Far** said, "I've got another surprise for you."

"What is it?" Nikolai asked.

"Not until tomorrow. Now you're going to help **Mor** in the kitchen. There's **bøf med løg** tonight." The Danish burgers covered with onion gravy were the boys' favorite.

Early the next morning Nikolai awoke to find a note by his bed. It read: 'Dear Nikolai, I'll meet you on the red boat. Love, **Far**.' No sooner was Nikolai dressed than he was out of the front door, heading up the street. **Far** was already onboard the boat when Nikolai got there.

"Godmorgen, good morning, Nikolai. A lovely day." Father smiled.

"What's the surprise, **Far**?" Nikolai asked eagerly.

"This boat now belongs to us. I've been saving up for years to buy it."

"Really!" Nikolai's eyes beamed.

"There's a lot of work to be done before she can go to sea. But I don't think you'll mind that. And Lars has offered to help us as well."

"It's... it's ours!" Nikolai could hardly talk. He was so excited. He ran up and down the length of the boat. **Far** stood by the ship's wheel and watched Nikolai with a big smile on his face.

"Thank you, **tusind tak**, **Far**," Nikolai said laughing. He held onto the ship's wheel and breathed deeply the salty air. Nikolai was very happy and wanted nothing more.

"Dear friends, let us love one another, for love comes from God. Everyone who loves has been born of God and knows God. There is no fear in love. But perfect love drives out fear."

1 John 4:7 and 18 (NIV)